D E F G

K L M

Q R S T

X Y Z

# A Visit to Grandad:
# An African
# A B C

**Sade Fadipe**
Illustrated by Shedrach Ayalomeh

CASSAVA REPUBLIC

$A$ is for Adanah
and my school is on break.

*B* is for bags
packed with things I'm going to take.

*C* is for camera
to take pictures of my stay.

*D* is for Dad
who drives me all the way.

*E* is for eagles
flying high above the trees.

*F* is for forest

sunlight shining through the leaves.

*G* is for gate.
We enter Grandad's yard.

**H** is for hugs.
I squeeze him really hard!

*I* is for insects
that dance around my plate.

*J* is for juice.

I have orange juice with my dates.

*K* is for kitchen.
I sweep it with a broom.

*L* is for lantern
sparkling brightly in my room.

*M* is for mosquito net.
There's one around my bed.

*N* is for night with lots of stars above my head.

*O* is for onions
Grandad slices for my eggs.

*P* is for pump.
We fetch water in our kegs.

Q is for queen.
We make crowns out of hay.

*R* is for rake.
We clear all the twigs away.

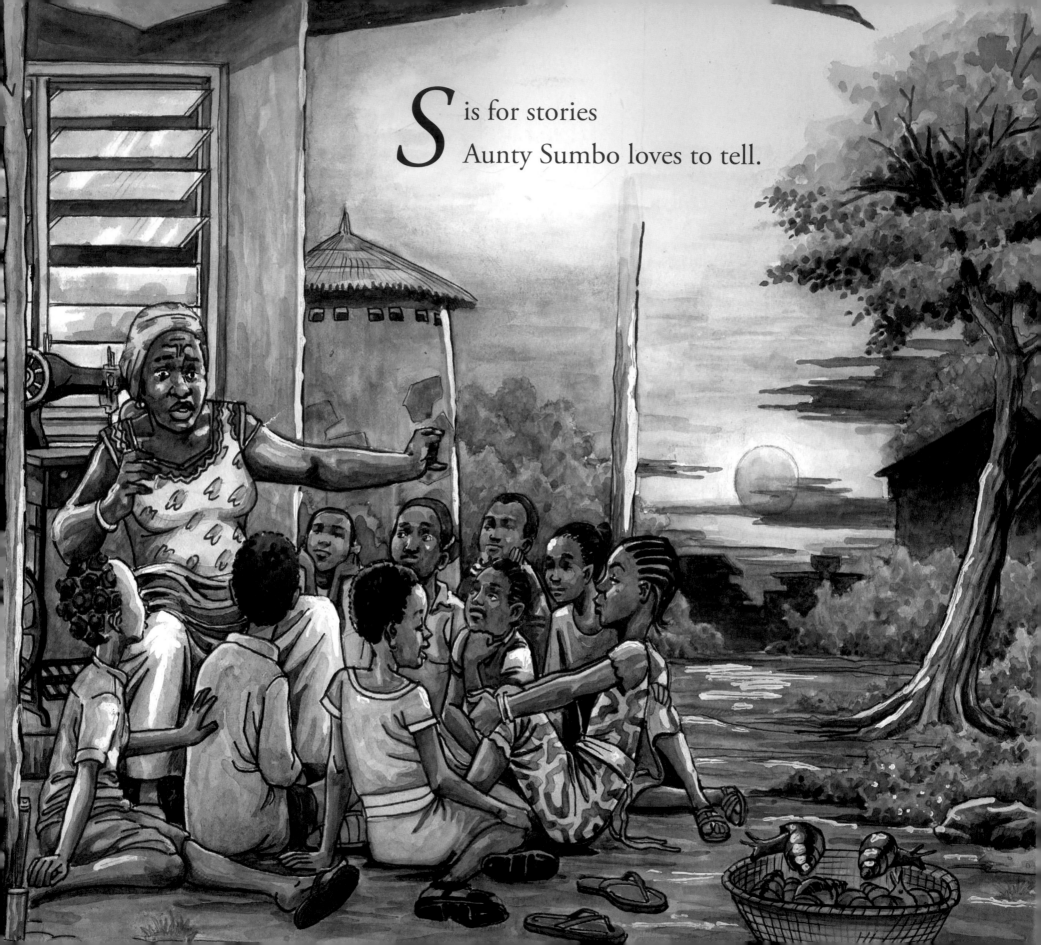

*S* is for stories
Aunty Sumbo loves to tell.

*T* is for table.
Is that fried plantain I smell?

*U* is for umbrella.

We love to splash in puddles.

*V* is for van.

I run to Mum for cuddles.

W is for waving.
Now I feel quite sad.

X is for xylophone.
A gift to make me glad.

$Y$ is for yams.
Lots of tubers for my mum.

Z is for Zainab.
I hope next time you can come.

**Did you manage to spot all the other objects starting with the same letter on each page?**
**Check the index below to see if there is anything you missed!**

**A:** Adanah, aeroplane, African necklace, apple

**B:** bag, ball, balloons, bananas, basket, bear, binoculars, blanket, blocks, blue room, books, box, bracelets, braids, broom, brush, bucket, bulb

**C:** cactus, camera, car, cat, chicks, comb, cup

**D:** Dad, dogs, drums

**E:** eagles, easel, eggs, electronics shop, elephant

**F:** falcon, fish, fisherman, flowers, forest

**G:** garden, gate, goat, Grandad, grass, guitar

**H:** hammer, hat, hens, hoe, horse, house, hugs

**I:** ice, ink, insects, iron, ivory

**J:** jacket, jar, jet, jug, juice

**K:** kerosene drum, kettle, keys, kitchen, knife

**L:** ladder, lantern, lion

**M:** magnifying glass, mask, mat, mirror, mosquito net

**N:** net, night, notebook, November

**O:** onions, oranges, oven

**P:** palm tree, people, pigeons, plants, pole, puddle, pump

**Q:** quail, queen

**R:** rake, red, reeds, rock, rope

**S:** sandals, sewing machine, shovel, sky, slippers, snails, stories, Sumbo (Aunty), sunset

**T:** table, tambourine, teapot, tire, tomatoes, torch (flashlight)

**U:** umbrella

**V:** van, vegetables, veranda, vest, vines

**W:** whistle, windscreen, wipers, woman, wrapping paper

**X:** xylophone

**Y:** yams, yellow curtains, yogurt

**Z:** Zainab

# More Children's Books from Cassava Republic Press

### Hair, it's a Family Affair!

Join Macy as she takes us on a journey through all the different hairstyles in her family, from big Afros to purple hair, and everything in between! A celebration of black hair through the vibrant and varied hairstyles found in a single family.

ISBN: 978-1911115137

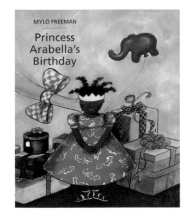

### Princess Arabella's Birthday

Ruby-encrusted roller skates, a golden bicycle, a stuffed mouse, a cuddly mouse, a tea set, a doll's pram carriage? No, Princess Arabella wants something different for her birthday: an elephant. But will she get what she wants?

ISBN: 978-1911115373

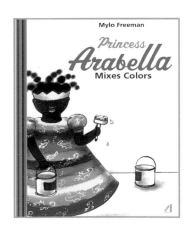

### Princess Arabella Mixes Colors

Princess Arabella thinks her room is boring. So she decides she's going to do something about that – all by herself. She mixes up some paint and in no time at all her room looks fabulous. A delightful picture book, with fun information about mixing colors.

ISBN: 978-1911115366

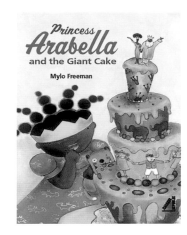

### Princess Arabella and the Giant Cake

It is almost Granny's birthday and Princess Arabella and her friends set out to bake the most DELICIOUS and most GIGANTIC cake in the entire world. But who will be the winner – Princess Arabella, Prince Mimoen, Princess Sophie or Princess Ling? And what is that surprise in the Giant Cake?!

ISBN: 978-1911115663

### Every Girl is a Princess

In this book, you'll meet princesses from all over the world. They all have their favorite animal and their own crown. But who fits the remaining crown? A cheerful and colorful picture book that shows that a little princess (or prince) hides in every child.

ISBN: 978-1911115380

A Cassava Republic Press edition. First published in the USA in 2019.
First published in the UK in 2016

Text by © Sade Fadipe 2015
Illustration by ©Shedrach Ayalomeh 2015
Edited by Laura Atkins
Design by Charlotte Rodenstedt

ISBN: 978-1-911115-81-6

www.cassavarepublic.biz